Bramble
and Maggie
SNOW DAY

Jessie Haas
illustrated by Alison Friend

To Michael, and to plow guys everywhere.
Many thanks!
J. H.

For Kelly and her unusual chickens
A. F.

Candlewick Sparks®. Candlewick Sparks is a registered trademark of Candlewick Press, Inc.

Text copyright © 2016 by Jessie Haas
Illustrations copyright © 2016 by Alison Friend

First paperback edition 2017

Library of Congress Catalog Card Number 2016947249
ISBN 978-0-7636-7364-2 (hardcover)
ISBN 978-0-7636-9780-8 (paperback)

17 18 19 20 21 22 TLF 10 9 8 7 6 5 4 3 2

Printed in Dongguan, Guangdong, China

This book was typeset in Dante.
The illustrations were done in gouache.

Candlewick Press
99 Dover Street
Somerville, Massachusetts 02144

visit us at www.candlewick.com

CHAPTER ONE

Storm Coming

The sky was white.

The air was cold and still.

Snowflakes tickled Bramble's back.

Bramble shook herself. The snowflakes
flew up in the air. They drifted down again.

The snowflakes were slow, but people
were in a hurry.

Maggie put extra hay in the hen's nest. She pulled a tarp over Bramble's hay pile.

KA-CRACK!

Mr. Dingle stapled plastic to his henhouse. "Big storm coming," he called. "Does that horse need a blanket?"

"No," Maggie said. "Her long hair will keep her warm."

2

That was what her big horse book said.

But was Bramble really warm enough?

Maggie reached up under Bramble's

mane. "Oh, you're *so* warm!"

Being warm was
not the problem.
Bramble bucked.

She rolled on the
ground.

The snowflakes
kept coming. So did
the tickles.

Bramble plunged
into her stall. She
went to the back,
where no snowflake
could touch her.

4

"That horse is wild," said Mr. Dingle.

"She must know a storm is coming."

"The storm is *here*!" said Maggie.

"It will get worse," said Mr. Dingle. "Got bottled water? If the power goes out, your water pump won't work."

"I'll ask," Maggie said. She ran to the house.

"Will we have enough water for Bramble?"
Maggie asked. "Horses drink ten gallons of
water every day!"

"We'll fill up the bathtub," Dad said.
"Then we'll have plenty of water, even for
Bramble. Now, what goes
on that shopping list?"

"Flashlight batteries," Mom said.

"Marshmallows," Maggie said.

"Marshmallows?" Mom asked.

"Yes," Maggie said. "We'll probably have a snow day tomorrow. I'll stay home from school and play outside with Bramble. I'll need marshmallows for hot cocoa."

"True," Mom said. "We have to be ready."

Bramble watched everyone work. She
watched the snow get deeper. She could
hear the wind. It was a long way off, but it
was coming.

"Supper time, Bramble," Maggie said.
"Here's some extra hay. My book says
extra hay helps horses stay warm in cold
weather."

Maggie tried to
push the stall door
closed. It would not
latch. Snow was
keeping it open just
a crack.

"That's okay," Maggie said.
"Bramble, you're a smart horse. I know
you'll stay inside."

She gave Bramble a kiss. "Sleep tight. I'll
see you in the morning."

CHAPTER TWO

Open Door

Bramble ate her hay. Outside, the wind whispered. Then it whooshed. Soon it started to howl.

Bramble looked out her door. The night was white and wild.

Bramble's legs wanted to move.

The stall was very small. Her legs could not move enough in there.

The snowflakes tickled her ears. Bramble turned away from her door. She ate more hay.

She took a drink. She poked the hen with her nose.

The hen stayed asleep.

Bramble couldn't sleep. She looked out again.

Cold, yes. Tickly, yes. But the storm was exciting.

Bramble *had* to be out in it. She leaned on her door.

The door moved, just a little.

Bramble leaned harder. The door opened
wide.

Bramble stepped outside. The snow was already deep. The lights in the house seemed far away. Snowflakes landed on Bramble's ears. She shook them off. More landed. They came so fast now, they didn't even tickle.

Bramble trudged to the fence. She walked along it. Snow packed under her feet. It made Bramble feel tall. It made everything else look shorter.

Now Bramble came to some tracks. Big
tracks. Deep tracks. She put her head down
and sniffed.

Her tracks. She had walked all the way around the fence.

Her stall door was still open. Bramble could go back inside.

But she liked it out here. The snow
settled on her back, as thick as a blanket.
It kept her warm.

Bramble turned her tail to the wind.
She put her head down.

She was stronger than a storm. *It* was just air and snowflakes.

She was a *horse*.

Maggie stared out the window. The night was white. She couldn't see Bramble's stall. She couldn't see Mr. Dingle's house. She could only see snow.

"I hope Bramble is okay out there."

Mom opened the big horse book.

ICE-AGE HORSES

Thick hair keeps out the cold.

Large nostrils warm the air.

Dig with their hooves for grass.

"Horses lived through the Ice Age," Mom said. "Bramble is as safe and warm as we are."

24

Bramble *was* warm under her snow blanket.

The snowflakes hissed down, faster and faster.

A plow roared, far away.

Up the street, something crashed.

The lights in the houses went off. They stayed off.

CHAPTER THREE
Marshmallows

In the morning, Maggie looked outside.
Everything looked white and soft.
Everything looked strange. Bramble's
door was wide open.

"Where is Bramble?" Maggie said.
"Where is *Bramble?"*

Maggie pushed the door. It wouldn't open. Snow had drifted up against it.

"Mom! Dad! Bramble's door is open! She's gone! We have to find her! But the front door is stuck!"

"Don't worry, Maggie," Dad said. "I'll climb out a window if I have to. Brr! Let me get dressed first."

Outdoors Bramble opened her eyes.

Everything looked soft and white —

and *strange*.

Her fence was gone.

That white mountain — was that Mr.

Dingle's henhouse?

That snowy lump — was it her hay pile?

Bramble plodded to the lump. Usually the fence kept her from getting to it. But the fence was deep under the snow. Bramble could walk right over it.

She smelled hay. She dug with her hoof.

All she found was the tarp.

Twit-tweet-twit! Birds sang at the feeder. Bramble waded over. Walking through the deep snow made her hungry. The birdseed was dry and crunchy. But it was better than nothing.

"Bramble! *There* you are!"

Maggie stood inside the door. Why didn't she come out? Didn't she know it was breakfast time?

Bramble plowed to the front steps. Maggie shoved the door. It only opened a crack.

Maggie said, "Sorry, Bramble. I know you're hungry. But we're stuck. Here, have some of my breakfast."

Maggie got a handful of cereal. She squeezed her hand through the door. The cereal fell on the snow.

Bramble pushed her nose deep into the snow. She dug with her front hoof. She found every crumb.

Maggie pushed the door again. It opened a little wider.

Dad started to open a window.

"Wait," Maggie said. "This might work."

She got more cereal. She tossed it on the snow. Bramble dug again.

"I'll go get dressed," Maggie said.

Dad shoved the door hard. "I still can't get through."

"Maybe I can," Maggie said.

She squeezed through the door. *"Bramble!*
You saved us!" Maggie gave Bramble a huge
handful of cereal and a huge hug.

Then Maggie kicked more snow away.

Dad squeezed out. He shoveled the steps.

Maggie looked around. "I don't see Mr.
Dingle," she said. "I don't see anybody!"

"People must be stuck like we were,"
Dad said.

Maggie said, "Let's go get them out!"

First they went to Mr. Dingle's house.

"*Thank* you!" said Mr. Dingle. He gave
Bramble a doughnut. He gave everyone
else doughnuts, too. "I'll get my shovel
and help."

Bramble plowed to the next house, and
the next. Everyone was glad to see her.
Everyone was glad to have a horse in the
neighborhood.

Dad and Mr. Dingle built a fire in Mr. Dingle's yard.

Mom brought out cocoa and marshmallows. Other people brought teakettles and soup pots, hot dogs and eggs and cheese sandwiches.

Everyone asked if Bramble would like a taste.

Bramble *would* like a taste. Some things tasted good. Some tasted not so good.

Up the street, chain saws growled. The snowplow roared through. Next the power truck came. "We'll have the power on soon," the driver said.

"We're doing fine without it," said Mr. Dingle.

That afternoon Mom and Dad shoveled
the driveway. Maggie shoveled Bramble's
doorway and cleared off the hay pile.

"Time for more cocoa," Maggie said.

Dad yawned. "Time for a nap! Snow days are hard work!"

Maggie brought her cocoa outdoors. She brought the bag of marshmallows, too.

The sky was blue.

The sun was warm.

Water dripped slowly off the icicles.

"I love snow days," Maggie said. "Another marshmallow, Bramble?"